FIND
YOUR PATH

LOVE
WHO YOU
ARE

SHARE
YOUR LIGHT

EXPLORE
NEW THINGS

Can Princesses Become Astronauts?

Carmela LaVigna Coyle *Pictures by Mike Gordon*

MUDDY BOOTS
Guilford, Connecticut

Published by Muddy Boots

An imprint of The Rowman & Littlefield Publishing Group, Inc.
4501 Forbes Blvd., Ste. 200
Lanham, MD 20706
www.rowman.com

MuddyBootsBooks.com

Distributed by NATIONAL BOOK NETWORK

British Library Cataloguing-in-Publication Information available

Library of Congress Cataloging-in-Publication Data available

ISBN 978-1-63076-347-3 (hardcover)

ISBN 978-1-63076-348-0 (e-book)

Printed in China

For Bettye, who is on her own journey through the stars.
—clvc

For Caiden and Carter, my budding artists!
—MG

Can a princess grow up to be anything?

As long as it's something
that makes her heart sing.

Can a princess become an astronaut?

I simply can't think of a reason why not.

Do astronauts go on journeys to Mars?

Princesses always reach for the stars.

Will I study birdies at the South Pole?

Maybe you'll lead a penguin patrol!

Can I be a coach? Or sell peanuts and pop?

Or you can be a Mama who's playing shortstop.

I might be the captain on a deep sea mission.

So, where should we go
on your first expedition?

Can I get a job as a spring flower fairy?

That kind of job sounds extraordinary.

Can a princess become a yoga instructor?

Or firefighter! Or doctor! Or concert conductor!

Do princesses play with gadgets and gears?
Some of them grow up to be engineers.

Can you make a gismo to help others somehow?

Look at this robot I invented just now!

Can a princess grow up
to be president?

She'd get my support a thousand percent.

Can a princess learn how to be a good cook?

Maybe I'll write The Royal Cookbook.

Can a princess grow up to be a librarian?

Or park ranger! Or builder! Or veterinarian!

Do you think everyone will like my fine art?

How could they not when you paint from your heart?

Maybe someday I will be QUEEN!

THAT *would be a sight to be seen.*

For now I'm cozy
just being me.

That's who I hope you always will be.

Where's YOUR rocket going?